The 12 Days of Halloween

by Jenna Lettice • illustrated by Colleen Madden

A Random House PICTUREBACK® Book

Random House New York

Text copyright © 2017 by Jenna Lettice. Cover art and interior illustrations copyright © 2017 by Colleen Madden.
All rights reserved. Published in the United States by Random House Children's Books, a division of
Penguin Random House LLC, 1745 Broadway, New York, NY 10019. Pictureback, Random House,
and the Random House colophon are registered trademarks of Penguin Random House LLC.
randomhousekids.com
Library of Congress Control Number: 2016001652
ISBN: 978-0-399-55731-6 (trade) — ISBN 978-0-399-55732-3 (ebook)
MANUFACTURED IN CHINA 10 9 8 7 6 5 4 3 2 1

On the **first** day of Halloween,
what showed up at our door?

One very eager trick-or-treater.

On the **second** day of Halloween,
what showed up at our door?

Two stuffed scarecrows
and one very eager trick-or-treater.

On the **third** day of Halloween,
what showed up at our door?

Three jack-o'-lanterns,
Two stuffed scarecrows,
and one very eager trick-or-treater.

On the **fourth** day of Halloween,
what showed up at our door?

Four scary costumes,
Three jack-o'-lanterns,
Two stuffed scarecrows,
and one very eager trick-or-treater.

On the **fifth** day of Halloween,
what showed up at our door?

Five bags of candy!
Four scary costumes,
Three jack-o'-lanterns,
Two stuffed scarecrows,
and one very eager trick-or-treater.

On the **sixth** day of Halloween,
what showed up at our door?

Six ghosts a-spooking,
Five bags of candy!
Four scary costumes,
Three jack-o'-lanterns,
Two stuffed scarecrows,
and one very eager trick-or-treater.

On the **seventh** day of Halloween,
what showed up at our door?

Seven spiders crawling,
Six ghosts a-spooking,
Five bags of candy!
Four scary costumes,
Three jack-o'-lanterns,
Two stuffed scarecrows,
and one very eager trick-or-treater.

On the **eighth** day of Halloween,
what showed up at our door?

Eight black cats hissing,
Seven spiders crawling,
Six ghosts a-spooking,
Five bags of candy!
Four scary costumes,
Three jack-o'-lanterns,
Two stuffed scarecrows,
and one very eager trick-or-treater.

Where's my kitty?
Oh, Mr. Cuddles!
My kitty loves cheese fishies!
Eight kittens. You can't miss 'em.
Mrowww?
Have you seen our cats
Hey.
Okay, where are they?

On the **ninth** day of Halloween,
what showed up at our door?

Nine witches cackling,
Eight black cats hissing,
Seven spiders crawling,
Six ghosts a-spooking,
Five bags of candy!
Four scary costumes,
Three jack-o'-lanterns,
Two stuffed scarecrows,
and one very eager trick-or-treater.

On the **tenth** day of Halloween,
what showed up at our door?

Ten werewolves howling,
Nine witches cackling,
Eight black cats hissing,
Seven spiders crawling,
Six ghosts a-spooking,
Five bags of candy!
Four scary costumes,
Three jack-o'-lanterns,
Two stuffed scarecrows,
and one very eager trick-or-treater.

On the **eleventh** day of Halloween,
what showed up at our door?

Eleven vampires grinning,
Ten werewolves howling,

OCTOBER 30TH

Nine witches cackling,
Eight black cats hissing,
Seven spiders crawling,
Six ghosts a-spooking,
Five bags of candy!
Four scary costumes,
Three jack-o'-lanterns,
Two stuffed scarecrows,
and one very eager trick-or-treater.

On the **twelfth** day of Halloween,
what showed up at our door?

Twelve devils plotting,
Eleven vampires grinning,
Ten werewolves howling,
Nine witches cackling,
Eight black cats hissing,
Seven spiders crawling,
Six ghosts a-spooking,
Five bags of candy!
Four scary costumes,
Three jack-o'-lanterns,
Two stuffed scarecrows . . .

and one very eager trick-or-treater.

Happy Halloween!